VERY LAST FIRST TIME

Eva Padlyat lived in a village on Ungava Bay in northern Canada. She was Inuit, and ever since she could remember she had walked with her mother on the bottom of the sea. It was something the people of her village did in winter when they wanted mussels to eat.

Today, something very special was going to happen. Today, for the very first time in her life, Eva would walk on the bottom of the sea alone.

VERY LAST FIRST TIME

BY Jan Andrews
ILLUSTRATED BY Ian Wallace

A Margaret K. McElderry Book
ATHENEUM   NEW YORK

ALSO WRITTEN AND ILLUSTRATED BY Ian Wallace
Chin Chiang and the Dragon's Dance
(A Margaret K. McElderry Book)

Margaret K. McElderry Books
Macmillan Publishing Company
866 Third Avenue
New York, NY 10022
Collier Macmillan Canada, Inc.

Printed and bound in Hong Kong by Everbest Printing Co., Ltd.

Library of Congress Card Catalog Number: 85-71606
ISBN 0-689-50388-1

5 7 9 11 13 15 17   20 18 16 14 12 10 8 6

Eva got ready. Standing in their small, warm kitchen, Eva looked at her mother and smiled.

"Shall we go now?"

"I think we'd better."

"We'll start out together, won't we?"

Eva's mother nodded. Pulling up their warm hoods, they went out.

Beside the house there were two sleds, each holding a shovel, a long ice-chisel and a mussel pan. Dragging the sleds behind them, they started off.

Eva and her mother walked through the village. Snow lay white as far as the eye could see — snow, but not a single tree, for miles and miles on the vast northern tundra. The village was off by itself. There were no highways, but snowmobile tracks led away and disappeared into the distance.

Down by the shore they met some friends and stopped for a quick greeting.

They had come at the right time. The tide was out, pulling the sea water away, so there would be room for them to climb under the thick ice and wander about on the seabed.

Eva and her mother walked carefully over the bumps and ridges of the frozen sea. Soon they found a spot where the ice was cracked and broken.

"This is the right place," Eva said.

After shoveling away a pile of snow, she reached for the ice-chisel. She worked it under an ice hump and, heaving and pushing with her mother's help, made a hole.

Eva peered down into the hole and felt the dampness of the air below. She breathed deep to catch the salt sea smell.

"Good luck," Eva's mother said.

Eva grinned. "Good luck yourself."

Her eyes lit up with excitement and she threw her mussel pan into the hole. Then she lowered herself slowly into the darkness, feeling with her feet until they touched a rock and she could let go of the ice above.

In a minute, she was standing on the seabed.
　　Above her, in the ice hole, the wind whistled. Eva
struck a match and lit a candle. The gold-bright flame
shone and glistened on the wet stones and pools
at her feet.

She held her candle and saw strange shadow shapes
around her. The shadows formed a wolf, a bear, a seal
sea-monster. Eva watched them, then she remembered.
"I'd better get to work," she said.

Lighting three more candles, she carefully wedged them between stones so she could see to collect mussels. Using her knife as a lever, she tugged and pried and scraped to pull the mussels off the rocks. She was in luck. There were strings of blue-black mussel shells whichever way she turned.

Alone — for the first time.

Eva was so happy she started to sing. Her song echoed around, so she sang louder. She hummed far back in her throat to make the echoes rumble. She lifted up long strings of mussels and let them clatter into her pan.

Soon her mussel pan was full, so she had time to explore.

She found a rock pool that was deep and clear. Small shrimps in the water darted and skittered in the light from her candle. She stopped to watch them. Reaching under a ledge, she touched a pinky-purple crab. The fronds of the anemones on the ledge tickled her wrist.

Beyond the rock pool, seaweed was piled in thick, wet, shiny heaps and masses. Eva scrambled over the seaweed, up and onto a rock mound. Stretching her arms wide, tilting her head back, she laughed, imagining the shifting, waving, lifting swirl of seaweed when the tide comes in.

The tide!
Eva listened. The lap, lap of the waves sounded
louder and nearer. Whoosh and roar and whoosh again.

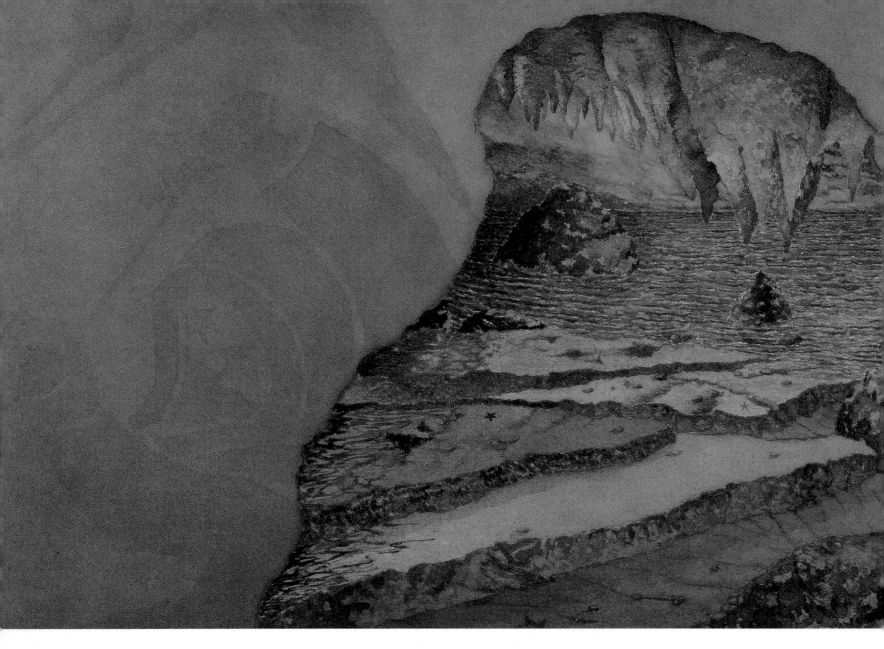

Eva jumped off the rock, stumbled — and her candle
dropped and sputtered out. She had gone too far. The
candles she had set down between the stones had
burned to nothing. There was darkness — darkness
all around.

"Help me!" she called, but her voice was swallowed.
"Someone come quickly."

   Eva closed her eyes. Her hands went to her face. She
could not bear to look.

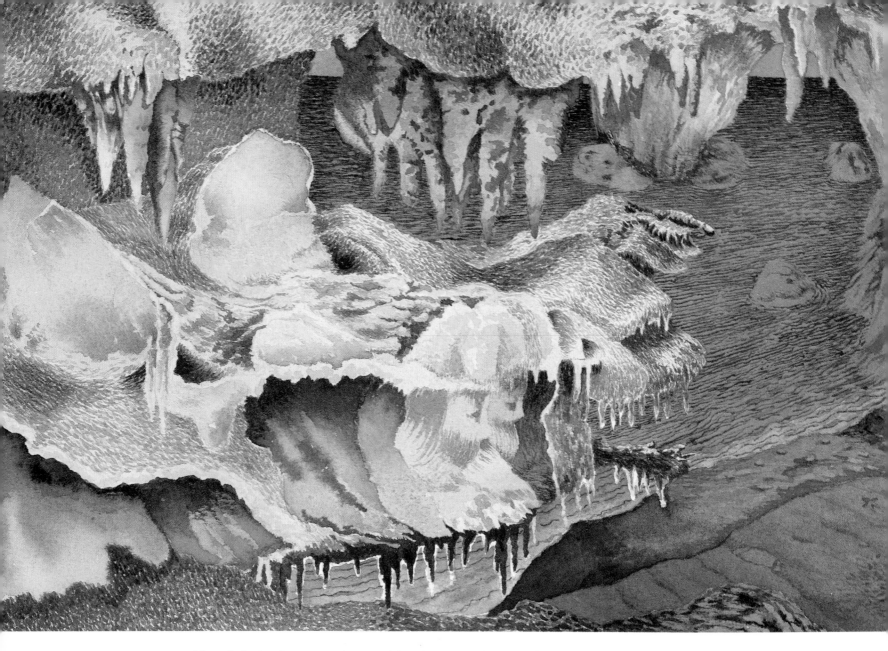

She felt in her pockets. She knew she had more
candles there, but she could not seem to find them.
The tide was roaring louder and the ice shrieked and
creaked with its movement.

Eva's hands groped deeper. She took a candle out
at last and her box of matches, but her fingers were
shaking and clumsy. For a long, forever moment,
she could not strike the match to light the candle.

The flame seemed pale and weak.

Eva walked slowly, fearfully, peering through the
shadows, looking for her mussel pan.

At last, she found it and ran stumbling to the
ice-hole. Then, looking up, Eva saw the moon in the sky.
It was high and round and big. Its light cast a circle
through the hole onto the seabed at her feet.

Eva stood in the moonlight. Her parka glowed.
Blowing out her candle, she slowly began to smile.

By the time her mother came, she was dancing. She

was skipping and leaping in and out of the moonglow
circle, darkness and light, in and out.

"Eva," her mother called.

"I'm here," she called back. "Take my mussel pan."
Eva scrambled onto a rock and held the pan up high to
her mother. Then her mother's hands reached down and
pulled her up, too, through the hole.

Squeezing her mother's hand, Eva saw the moon, shining on the snow and ice, and felt the wind on her face once more.

"That was my last very first — my very last *first* time — for walking alone on the bottom of the sea," Eva said.